Giggles and More!

SESAME STREET

with Abby and Friends

The DALMATIAN PRESS and PIGGY TOES PRESS names and logos are trademarks of Dalmatian Publishing Group, Atlanta, Georgia 30329. No part of this book may be reproduced or copied in any form without written permission from the copyright owner. All rights reserved.

Printed in the U.S.A.
ISBN: 1-61524-233-3

10 11 12 13 B&M 35782 10 9 8 7 6 5 4 3 2 1
Sesame Street Softcover Treasury: Giggles and More!

contents

Storybook ABCs

By P.J. Shaw   Illustrated by Tom Brannon

A
Apple

Abby, Abby, quite Cadabby,
How does your alphabet grow?
With ABC—then letters to Z!
Twenty-six, all in a row.

The alphabet is amazing!

9

J

Jack

Jog and juggle! Jack, be quick!
Jack, jump over the candlestick!

Enough jogging, juggling, and jumping. I, Jack, am going back to beanstalks.

Old King Cole was a grouchy old soul,
And a grouchy old soul was he.
He called for some junk,
And he called for his skunk,
And he called his kazoo-players three.

13

L
Lamb

Prairie had a little lamb,
Little lamb, little lamb.
Prairie had a little lamb.
Its fleece was light as snow.

14

M
Mud

Messy Miss Muffet
Sat on a tuffet,
Eating some mud soufflé.
In marched a spider
To sit down beside her—
But she frightened that spider away!

15

O
Oven

P
Pie

Pat a pie, pat a pie, baker's man.
Make me a pie as fast as you can.
Pat it and prick it and mark it with **P**.
Put it in the oven for piggy and me!

17

Q
Queen

Oh, I quit.

The Queen of Hearts
Made quiche and tarts,
All on a quiet day.
The Knave of Hearts,
He stole those tarts
And quickly ran away!

23

ABBY CADABBY'S
Rhyme Time

By P.J. Shaw   Illustrated by Tom Leigh

Lumpkin, bumpkin, diddle-diddle dumpkin, zumpkin, frumpkin, pumpkin!

"As a fairy-in-training, I practice my magic tricks with rhymes—you know, words that end with the same sound, like **bat** and **cat**! Rhymes are so fun to find! I know—let's find some rhymes together. Hmmmm. What words rhyme with … **rhyme**?"

29

What words rhyme with **sheep**?
Noisy cars that go "**beep**"!
A ballet dancer's **leap**,
And a trash heap to **sweep**.

What words rhyme with **go**?
I bet that you **know**!
There's a boat you can **row**,
And cars that go *slooooow*.

What rhymes with **icky**?
Bubblegum that is **sticky**,
A game that is **tricky**,
And dogs who are **licky**.

33

Which words sound like **zap**?
Fairy wings going **flap**!
And the shoes that you **tap**
To the beat—as you **snap**!

Do some words rhyme with **stick**?
Yes! A house made of **brick**,
A soft baby **chick**,
Or a camera to **click**!

37

What rhymes with **tub**?
Well, there's **scrub-a-dub-dub**,
And a miniature **sub**,
Or one baby bear **cub**!

44

What rhymes with **nose**?
Snuffleupagus **toes**,
A swishy fish that **glows**!
And a slithery **hose**.

What words rhyme with **sloppy**,
Like Oscar's **Jalopy**?
Bunnies all **hoppy**
With ears that are **floppy**.

Let's find rhymes for **story**!
Like a lion who's **roar-y**,
A monster who's **snore-y**...
And space that's **explore-y**!

An itsy-bitsy pajama party!
Is that not adorable?

49

And last, what rhymes with **tabby**?
A blankie that's **shabby**,
A fairy named **Abby**,
And the family **Cadabby**!

Happy and Sad, Grouchy and Glad

By Constance Allen   Illustrated by Tom Brannon

Oh welcome, oh welcom
to our little play.
We are ever so glad
you could join us today!

We are going to talk about FEELINGS!
And so…please open the curtain
and on with the show!

We are two furry monsters,
one red and one blue.
We can count up to twenty
and tie our own shoes.
We can sing oh-so-sweetly—
OR SHOUT VERY LOUD!
Have you guessed how we feel?
We're both feeling PROUD!

Oh! See big plate of cookies
all gooey and sweet—
with big chocolate chips!
What time do we eat?

When me have some cookies,
that make me feel GLAD!

But when poor plate empty...
 (*Hmm. Maybe just one or two*
 to see how they taste.
 Mmmm! Delicious!
 Gobble, gobble!)
me feel very SAD!

To show you *my* feeling
I'll do a short dance.

I feel so EMBARRASSED
in polka-dot pants!

When Oscar's up late
and makes too much noise,
when people at play group
will not share their toys,
when my birdseed pancakes
turn out to be lumpy,
I sit in a corner
and feel really GRUMPY!

Pizza and ice cream,
my little pet fish,
my warm fuzzy blankie,
my favorite dish,
cute furry kitties,
and honey on toast—
these things are all nice,
but I LOVE MOMMY most!

63

Mumford's my name,
Many tricks I perform.
I pull rabbits from hats.
I can make a rainstorm!

A-LA-PEANUT-BUTTER
SANDWICHES!

Good heavens, my rabbits
are extra-large-sized!
It's snowing, not raining—
even I feel SURPRISED!

I'm Shelley the Turtle.
I'll make my rhyme brief,
for I'm shaking and trembling
up here like a leaf!
I feel awfully SHY,
in case you can't tell,
so if nobody minds,
I'll go back in my shell.

When your crayons get broken,
you've lost your new shoe,
your picnic gets rained on
you've nothing to do,
you stub your big toe,
and you have to yell OUCH!
Well, what could be better?
You'll feel like a GROUCH!

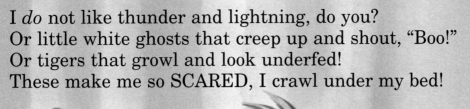

I *do* not like thunder and lightning, do you?
Or little white ghosts that creep up and shout, "Boo!"
Or tigers that growl and look underfed!
These make me so SCARED, I crawl under my bed!

When we're feeling HAPPY,
we stand on our heads
and we dance all around
and we jump on our beds!
We sing tra-la-la
and we laugh ho-ho-ho!
When we're feeling HAPPY,
we let the world know!

And that is the ending of our little play.
We thank you for sharing our feelings today!

What Makes You Giggle?

By P.J. Shaw   Illustrated by Tom Brannon

What makes you giggle,
What gives you a grin?
Big Bird in a tutu doing a spin!

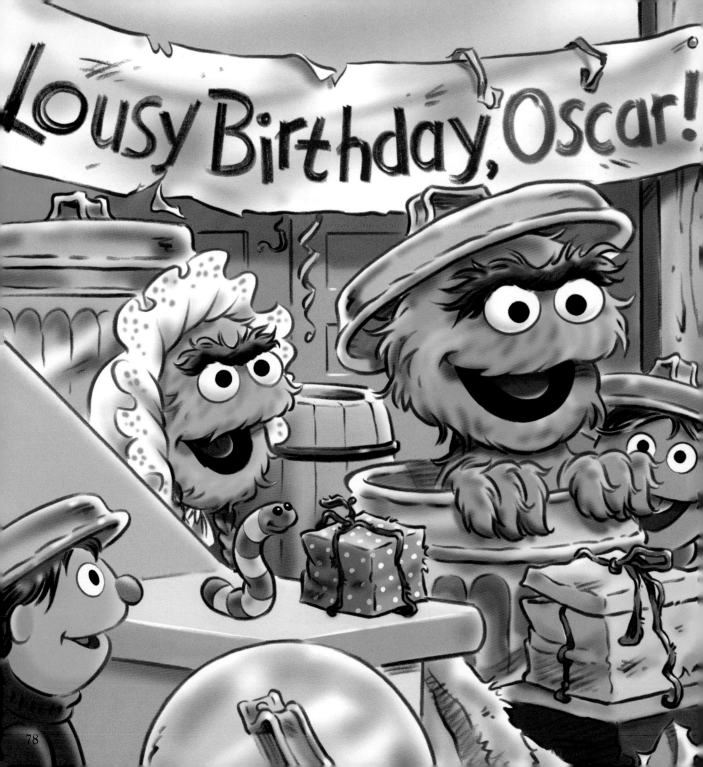

What makes you chuckle,
Or tickles your tummy?
A grouch birthday party—
Where presents are crummy!

Do giraffes give you laughs
On a trip to the zoo?
Or how about chimps?
Monkey-see, monkey-do!

A Snuffleupagus race
Might just give you a smile.
They *galumph* to the finish.
Alice wins by a mile!

What makes you laugh,
What makes you giggle?
A monstrous contest
For noses that wiggle!

What makes you whoop,
Makes you squeal with delight?
A day at the pool,
When the water's just right.

Dive rings and water wings,
Snorkels and masks.
Flippers and floaties,
And fountains that splash!

What makes you snicker,
Guffaw or tee-hee?
A neighborhood cookout
At Nani Bird's tree?

Make-your-own cupcakes
With milk-chocolate chips?
Maybe strawberries, raisins,
Or cinnamon bits....

Coconut, sprinkles,
Or butterscotch drops,
And pink-and-white frosting
To plop right on top.

What makes you goofy?
What makes you titter?
To trade silly faces
With Curly Bear's sitter!

A Twiddlebugs' picnic
With muffins and honey?

Or...an all-Grover rodeo—
Now, *that* would be funny!

What makes you giggle—
Makes you feel really good?
Just a regular day,
In your own neighborhood!